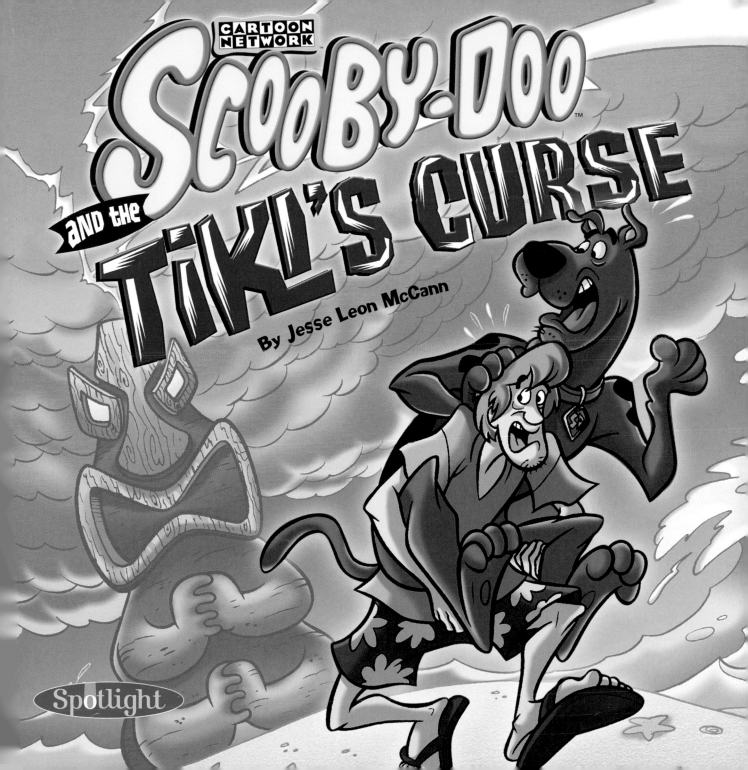

visit us at www.abdopublishing.com

Reinforced library bound edition published in 2010 by Spotlight, a division of the ABDO Group, 8000 West 78th Street, Edina, Minnesota 55439. Spotlight produces high-quality reinforced library bound editions for schools and libraries. Published by agreement with Warner Bros.—A Time Warner Company. The stories, characters, and incidents mentioned are entirely fictional. All rights reserved. Used under authorization.

For my best friend, Nancy.

Printed in the United States of America, Melrose Park, Illinois.
092009
012010

 PRINTED ON RECYCLED PAPER

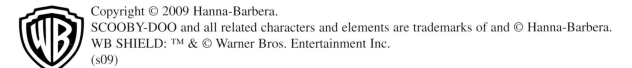
Special thanks to Duendes del Sur for cover and interior illustrations.

Library of Congress Cataloging-in-Publication Data

McCann, Jesse Leon.
  Scooby-Doo and the tiki's curse / by Jesse Leon McCann ; [cover and interior illustrations, Duendes del Sur]. -- Reinforced library bound ed.
     p. cm.
  ISBN 978-1-59961-680-3
  I. Duendes Del Sur (Firm) II. Scooby-Doo (Television program) III. Title.
  PZ7.M47835Scu 2010
  [Fic]--dc22

                              2009031243

All Spotlight books are reinforced library binding
and manufactured in the United States of America.

Scooby and his Mystery, Inc. friends were visiting Hawaii. They were planning to ride their bikes in a race for charity. They were also planning to have some fun!

Sand surfing over the black sands of Oneuli Beach was a *whole lot* of fun!

"Roo hoo!" Scooby-Doo rode the wind, *major kine* style!

"The sand pebbles are made of black lava basalt," Velma explained. "It reflects the sun, so put on your sunblock!"

5

Suddenly, the wind blew! The water churned! A huge, fearsome statue rose out of the water!

"Leave this place!" the statue boomed. "I, tiki god Pu'u Ola'i, demand it!"

Spitting fire, the tiki drew nearer. Everyone ran away as fast as they could!

Afterward, the gang wondered what the tiki was, and why it wanted everyone off the beach.

"Pu'u Ola'i doesn't just want everyone to leave the beach," said an eavesdropping old woman. "The legend says that it wants all strangers to leave Maui forever!"

Later, their host, Johnny Kopono,
drove the kids up the Hana Highway.
Johnny pointed to a man
passing them at a dangerous speed.
"That *babooze* is Cedric Pennington,
the millionaire. He wants to buy my
family's land, but we won't sell."

9

Johnny took them to the Seven Sacred Pools, one of the most beautiful spots in Hawaii.

"Like, this is what I call living!" Shaggy exclaimed.
"The only thing missing is a luau!"

"Reah! Reah!" Scooby-Doo licked his lips
hungrily.

11

But the angry monster tiki suddenly appeared, just as it had done on the beach.

"You will be destroyed!" the tiki bellowed. "You will feel my wrath!"

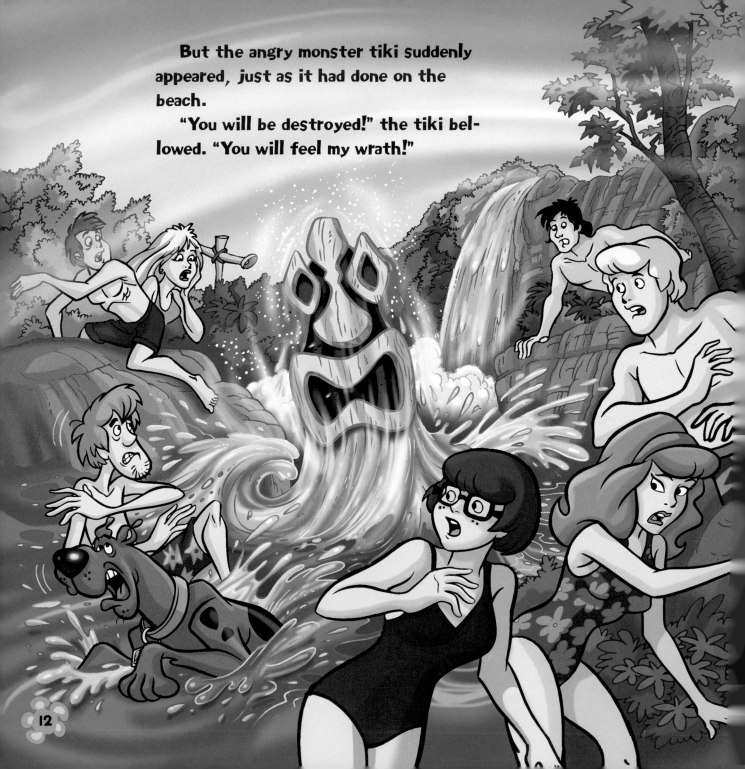

Shaggy and Scooby ran as fast as they could from the creepy tiki! They raced away from the pools and across a nearby pasture. The tiki chased them. "Doom! Doom!" it shouted.

"Zoinks!" yelled Shaggy.

"Relp! Relp!" cried Scooby.

That evening, the gang sat down to talk.
"I know this tiki is a fake," Fred said.
"Come on, gang! Let's solve this mystery!"
The kids went hiking around the area
where they'd seen the tiki. Velma thought
she'd spotted a clue, but when they got
closer, there was nothing there.

14

The next morning, it was time for the big charity bicycle race. The Mystery, Inc. gang forgot about the tiki menace and got ready for some serious fun!

Snobby Cedric Pennington wasn't having fun, though. Johnny still wouldn't sell his land.

Ready, set, go! **The racers were off, pedaling swiftly down the twisting, turning course of Hana Highway!**

"Like, faster, Scooby, we're in last place," Shaggy huffed. "Maybe we shouldn't have eaten those thirty pineapple-chili burgers until *after* the race!"

"Ruh-huh!" Scooby puffed.

But then the tiki appeared once more. "Doom! Doom on you!" it boomed.

"Look out!" Fred warned, but it was too late. The cyclists crashed their bikes!

"Jeepers!" cried Daphne.

Scooby and Shaggy cycled right through the tiki, off the road and into the ocean. *SPLASH!*

And just as suddenly as it had appeared, the tiki disappeared.

"Jinkies!" Velma exclaimed. She had seen something unusual. But when she blinked and looked again, it was gone.

Fred was sure Cedric was behind the tiki mystery, and wanted to catch him in the act. The gang trooped over to Cedric's house.

"Come see the beautiful Hula Sisters!" Velma announced loudly. She was trying to attract the tiki. Fred and Daphne hid in the bushes.

Cedric came out, and he wasn't very happy! "What is the meaning of this nonsense?"

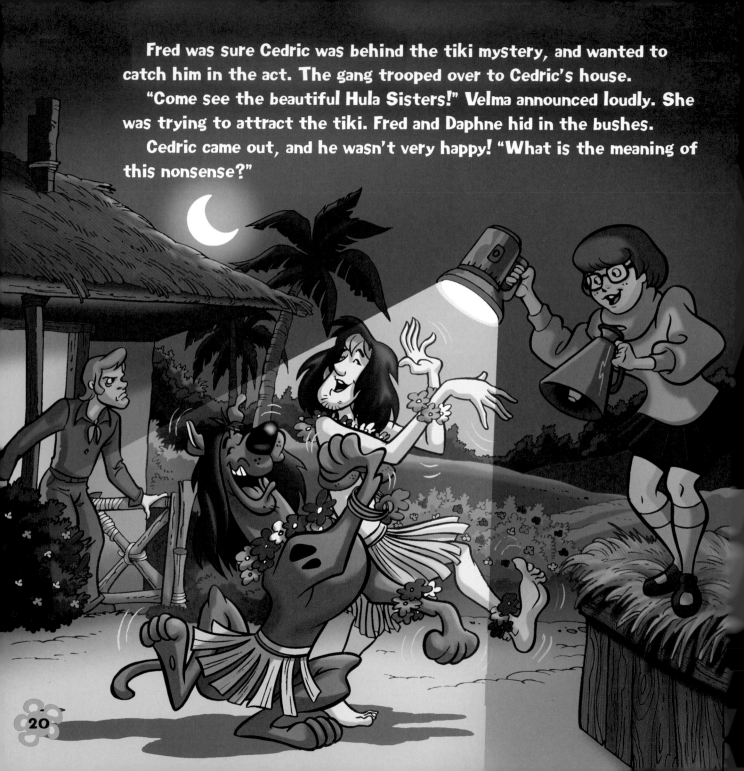

Just then, the terrifying tiki appeared again. "You have been warned! Now you must pay!"

It was clear that Cedric wasn't behind it after all. When he saw the tiki, he shrieked and ran away!

A sudden light came from above. The whole area lit up. The tiki became a harmless illusion projected upon flying grains of black sand. Their friend Johnny Kopono had solved the mystery!

"Curse you meddling kids and your nosy dog!"
screeched the old woman. "We wanted to frighten
everyone away! Then we could have bought this land
for next to nothing!"

The next morning, the police came and took the woman away. The charity bike race was rescheduled for the following day. This time, the race would be monster tiki-free!

"Like, now it's time for more fun in the sun!" Shaggy grinned. "Right, Scoob?"

"Right!" agreed Scooby-Doo. "Aloha-rooby-dooby-doo!"